D1459081

barcode →

FOR SADIE AND THE MOONDANCE DINER.

OSCAR AND ARABELLA
by Neal Layton
British Library Cataloguing in Publication Data
A catalogue record of this book is available from
the British Library.
ISBN 0340 79719 3 (HB)
ISBN 0340 79720 7 (PB)

Copyright © Neal Layton 2002

First edition published 2002
10 9 8 7 6 5

Published by Hodder Children's Books
a division of Hodder Headline Limited
338 Euston Road London NW1 3BH

Printed in Hong Kong

Oscar and Arabella

by Neal Layton

Oscar was a WOOLLY MAMMOTH.

And so was Arabella.

They liked snacking on leaves and berries,

but not too **MANY.**

They liked painting pictures,

OSCAR woz ERE

and getting in a MESS.

They liked
going exploring,

but didn't like the

DARK.

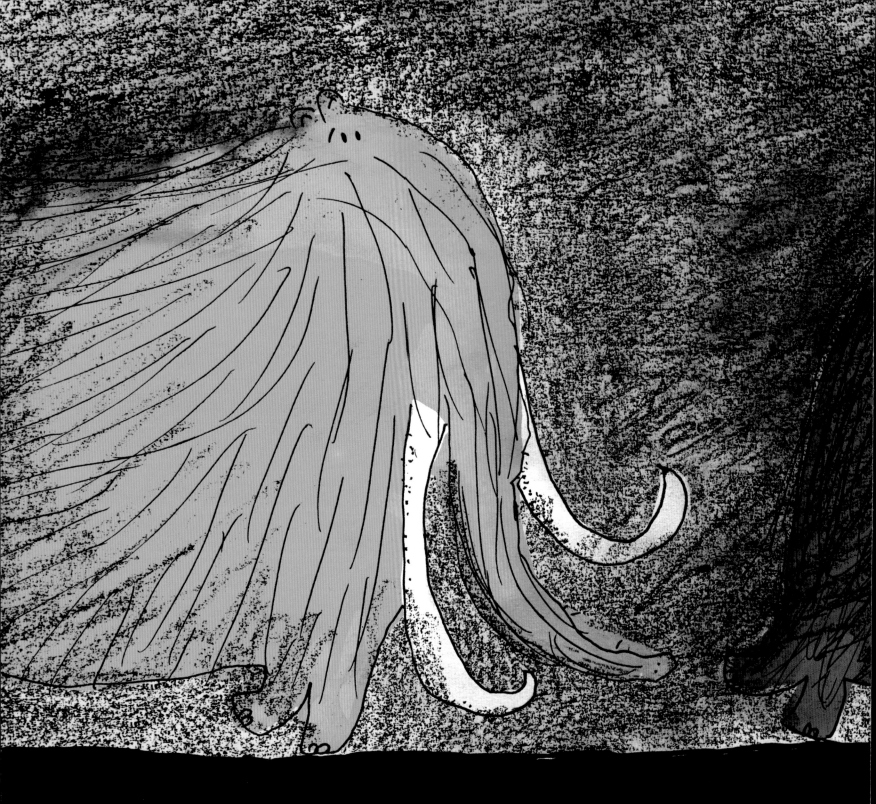

They liked adventures,

as long as they weren't SCARY.

They liked making friends,

but not with **wild** and dangerous animals.

They liked to keep **FIT** especially when

their lives depended on it.

They liked sliding on the ice,

as long as they didn't **FALL OVER.**

They liked
climbing trees,

but not too

HIGH.

They liked squirting water out of their trunks, because it was really good  FUN.

They liked to go sledging,

but not too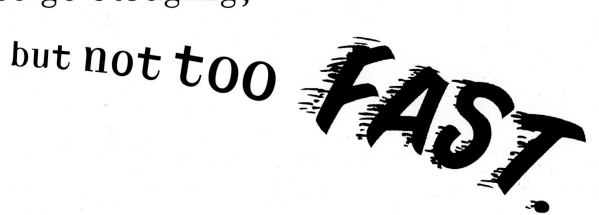

And, at the end of the day, they liked sitting around the campfire telling tales of their wild adventures to their friends, but not for too long...

Woolly Mammoth Facts

Woolly Mammoths ~~are~~ were cool.
They used to roam all over Eastern Europe,
Siberia and Colorado a long time ago in the
ice age. They stood 4-5 metres high
and weighed 20 tons or more. There were over 12 different species.
Their maximum lifespan was between 60-65 years.
They are now extinct
but their closest living relatives are ELEPHANTS,
and Elephants are really cool too.

TUSKS UP TO
5m LONG

HEIGHT
4-5m